Snowball
fight!

This
book
belongs
to:

_____

Dedicated to my two children, Aubree and Chase,
who love the warmth... and think the cold is OK sometimes too.

Meet January
©2021 Calendar Kids Books, LLC
Illustrations © April Martin

ISBN: 978-1-957161-01-3 (Paperback), 978-1-957161-02-0 (Hardback), 978-1-957161-00-6 (Ebook)
Library of Congress Control Number: 2021923173

For more information on the Calendar Kids® visit calendarkids.com or follow us on social media @thecalendarkids.

The Calendar Kids

meet
JANUARY

April Martin

This is January.

January loves to snuggle up
in bed. She loves to have pretend campfires
inside with her family. She loves to eat s'mores.
She loves her sleeping bag. She loves the
pretend stars on her bedroom wall too!

What January doesn't love, is the cold.
Her toes freeze. Her nose freezes.
Even her hair freezes rock solid.

Every time she wants to play outside, she has to put on layers
and layers of warm clothes. It takes forever to get ready.
After only a few minutes outside, she has to run in to warm up.

All winter break January got to sleep in, enjoy her new toys, and play with Flurry, her pet fox. Best of all, January got to celebrate the new year! Each day she marked off her calendar. Just four days left until school starts back. Her days off were coming to an end.

Finally, the day had come... there were no more days left of winter break and tomorrow she had to go back to school! Worst part of all, she had to walk to school in the cold.

Sunday	Monday	Tuesday	Wednesday	Thursday	Friday	Saturday
			~~1~~ New Year's Day	~~2~~	~~3~~	~~4~~
~~5~~	BACK 6 TO SCHOOL!	7	8	~~9~~	~~10~~	~~11~~
12	13	14 My Birthday!	15	16	17	18
19	20 Martin Luther King Jr. Day	21	22	23	24	25
26	27	28	29	30	31	

January's mom had a surprise for her the next morning to help get her excited for school. She made her favorite food, snowman pancakes, for breakfast. "Come on January! It's time to wake up and get ready for school," her mom yelled from downstairs.

January *pretended* to be asleep.

January *pretended* Flurry was sick.

January even *pretended* she was sick.

Her mom didn't fall for it.

"January, my snowflake, you get to see your friends again! You get to wish everyone a Happy New Year!" She said.

"It's time to go, come on, get up!"

So, January got up. She got dressed. She ate her pancakes. She got dressed even *more*. She said "bye" to Flurry, and she walked slowly to school. Each step she took she was more and more cold.

"Oh no", she thought, *"I can't feel my nose... I can't feel my toes... My hair even hurts!"*

Something was unusual about today. Today had to be the coldest day in the history of all cold days.

By the time January got to school she was frozen **solid**.
She couldn't move. She couldn't enjoy her friends.
She couldn't tell everyone about the new year.

All January could do was sit and sit and sit.
Oh, and she could drip and drip and drip!

Her whole class started to laugh at her. June and July thought for sure this was all a joke and asked,

"Are you sure you're really frozen?!"

Her closest friends, December and February, were the only ones not laughing. February reminded her that the winter will be over one day. December chimed in, "It's OK January, we understand."

"When it sits in the car all day!"

"When I eat it!"

"When the sun shines on it!"

Ms. Seasons spoke up and calmed the class.

"Now everyone. Let's think. What causes frozen things, like ice, to melt?"

Right!

"Now, what do they all have in common!? Heat!"

One by one the class got up and helped move January by the window. Thankfully, the sun was coming out. She waited until she could feel her nose. She waited until she could feel her toes. She waited until even her hair didn't hurt anymore. Finally, by lunch time, she was warm again.

You forgot your scarf!

CRAYON BIN

BIRDS
DOGS
CATS
REPTILES

GLUE

BLOCKS
Room 1A

HOW TO DRAW
DRAWING 4 KIDS
COLORING BOOK

RAINBOWS
CLOUDS
STORMS

"I sure wish winter was over!" January thought.

December and February were happy to talk to January again but couldn't figure out why she was so blue!

"It's just too cold! Look, even my hair is still frozen. I want to go play outside without freezing. I should just move to Florida where it's warm all year. I miss the trees and the grass and picking flowers."

February had an idea.

So, she whispered her idea to Ms.Seasons, and she agreed.

During lunch February and Ms. Seasons turned on the heaters.
They drew and they drew and they glued and they glued.

When they were finished, Ms. Seasons walked to the lunchroom and asked for January to come to the classroom.

TA-DA!

"Oh, February, you are the **best**!" January squealed.

February showed January where she could pick flowers. She sat and ate the rest of her lunch with her on the green, green grass. January was no longer blue! She was so cozy, so warm, and it felt like a warm spring day!

"Oh, I almost forgot!"
January announced. "Happy New year!"

On the way home December, January, and February built a snowman and snow kids. They made snowballs and snow cones.

Flurry joined in too!

"I guess winter can be fun too!" January thought...

...Until January was frozen solid once again...

My January Notebook

Special January birthdays or events in my family:

The best part about the month of January is...

January is the first month of the year.

The month after January is February.

January is a winter month.

January 31st is National Hot Chocolate Day.

Martin Luther King, Jr. holiday is celebrated on the third Monday in January every year.

January 1st is New Year's Day and marks the first day of a new year.

If you are born in January your birthstone is garnet.

The month of January has 31 days.

Discussion Questions

1. Did you know that not all areas get snow in January? Which places have snowy winters? Where can you find a warm climate all year?

2. Flurry is the name of January's fox. What does the word "flurry" mean during winter?

3. When February cheered January up, the book says that January was no longer blue. What did the author mean by that?

4. What is your favorite part about winter? Least favorite?

5. Have you ever played in the snow? What activities did you do that were fun? If not, what would you like to do in the snow?

6. What traditions does your family do on special days like New Year's Day?

7. Which of the four seasons can you find in Ms. Seasons hair? Her outfit?

Visit www.calendarkids.com for more resources.

Snowman Pancake Recipe

Homemade Pancake Mix:

4 cups of all-purpose flour
3 tablespoons baking powder
1 teaspoon salt
3 tablespoons sugar

How to make the dry mix:
Whisk all ingredients together
and store in a cool, dry place.

You will need:

1 cup of the pancake mix
1 cup of milk
1 egg
1 tablespoon of butter
1/2 cup chocolate chips

Directions:

1. Melt butter in the microwave. Heat up pan on medium heat.

2. Combine all pancake recipe ingredients except chocolate chips.

3. Pour 1/4 cup of batter onto the pan leaving room above, then quickly scoop
another 1/4 cup and pour a small amount of the scoop just above the first, and then again
pour an even smaller bit of mix at the top.

4. Drop chocolate chips onto your snowman. Two for the eyes, 3 buttons on the
belly, and 5 for the smile.

5. Cook about 3 to 4 minutes until the surface of the pancakes has bubbled and popped
and has firm edges. Flip and cook the other side another 2 minutes or until it is light golden
brown.

6. Top with syrup and enjoy!

meet APRIL

April Martin is a mother, military spouse, and teacher. While teaching her first grade class she discovered there were not many books to teach her students about the months of the year... that's where her very own name gave her an idea! She realized she could create characters named after the months of the year that her students could know and love. Time went by, LOTS of time, but her characters were still in her thoughts. Now, a mother herself, she wanted to finally bring the Calendar Kids to life. April knew all along the vision she had for her books and began to learn everything she could about writing and illustrating. April is a self-taught illustrator and always encourages others to explore new creative outlets. You never know, you could be just MONTHS away from creating something amazing!

More Facts About April

"First things first... YES, I was born in April! Whew, glad that's over with."

"My favorite season is fall, no wait, spring, no wait, fall. OK, yes, fall fo sure. No wait..."

"I LOVE to play in the snow. You can find me on the slopes! Unlike January, I love the cold. That's probably because I grew up in Florida!"

Made in the USA
Monee, IL
22 November 2023

47127901R00026